What Do You See
When You Shut Your Eyes?

Cynthia Zarin

Illustrated by
Sarah Durham

Houghton Mifflin Company
Boston 1998

For Rose, Anna, and Jack
— C.Z.

For Craig
— S.D.

Text copyright © 1998 by Cynthia Zarin
Illustrations copyright © 1998 by Sarah Durham

The text of this book is set in Garamond Condensed.
The illustrations are gouache and ink, reproduced in full color.

Library of Congress Cataloging-in-Publication Data

Zarin, Cynthia.
What do you see when you shut your eyes? / Cynthia Zarin; illustrated by Sarah Durham.
p. cm.
Summary: Dido, Peter, Lulu, and others exercise their senses, seeing a walking stick,
hearing the ice cream man, yelling, "Daddy!" and dreaming in their sleep.
ISBN 0-395-76507-2
[1. Senses and sensation—Fiction. 2. Stories in rhyme.]
I. Durham, Sarah, ill. II. Title.
PZ8.3.Z33Wh 1998
[E]—dc21 97-12012 CIP AC
CIP AC

Manufactured in the United States of America
WOZ 10 9 8 7 6 5 4 3 2 1

What do you see when you shut your eyes?

A bull with horns? A pig that flies?
Dido saw a skinny hen, Henry saw a snail,

Peter saw a green rabbit,
Lulu saw a nightingale—

What do you see when you shut your eyes?

What do you see when you peer around the door?

Wanda saw a walking stick, Freddie saw the floor,

Jack saw his shadow,
Anna saw the rain,

Rose saw her mama
coming home again—

What do you see when you peer around the door?

What do you hear when you listen hard?

Mimi heard the ice cream man,
Zack heard a car,

Nora heard a peacock screech,
Peach heard the snow,

Maximilian heard a ruckus,
Quint heard his hair grow—

What do you hear when you listen hard?

What can you find if you really look?

Rachel found a crocus,
Magda found a book,

Hannah found her sister,
Nushka found a feather,

Izzy found her temper, Tess found her sweater—

What do you find if you really look?

What do you yell when you yell really loud?

Matthew yelled "Daddy!" Mikey yelled "Slow down!"

Elliot yelled "Gotcha!"
Oliver yelled "Boo!"

Davis yelled "Watch out!"
Phoebe yelled "Cock-a-doodle-doo!"

What do you yell when you yell really loud?

What do you sing when you sing quietly?

Dora sang "Row, row, row your boat,"
Hilary sang "merrily,"

Raquel sang "Rub-a-Dub,"
Kate sang "Sweet Sixteen,"

then everybody all at once sang "Goodnight Irene!"

What do you sing when you sing quietly?

What do you see when you go to sleep?

Ariel saw her birthday, Tobias saw sheep,
Mollie saw a monster, Sophie saw her pillow,

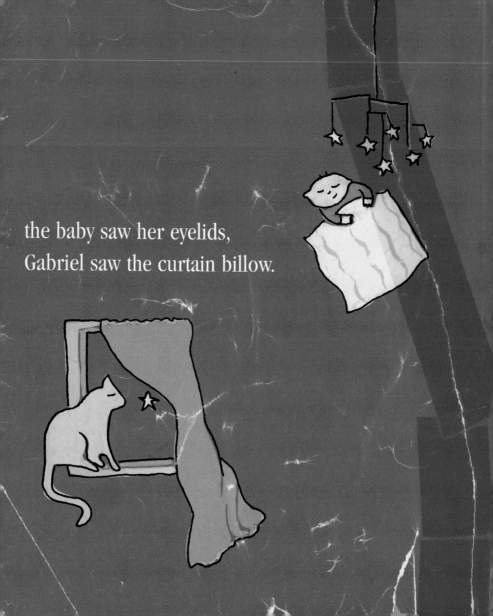

the baby saw her eyelids,
Gabriel saw the curtain billow.

Ssh.